THE TWIDDLEBUGS' DREAM HOUSE

Story by Pat Tornborg
Photographs by Alan Gelman

Miniatures by
Pat Tornborg and Alan Gelman

A SESAME STREET/GOLDEN PRESS BOOK

Published by Western Publishing Company, Inc.,
in conjunction with Children's Television Workshop.

The window box outside Jane's bedroom was a wonderful place for flowers. It was almost always sunny, with enough rain to make the flowers grow.

Mr. and Mrs. McTwiddle thought it was also a
wonderful place for young Twiddlebugs. Every
day, while their parents tended the little garden,
Tessie and Tiny played leap-bug among the flowers.

Each night, as the McTwiddles nestled into their cozy matchbox beds, Tiny asked, "What's inside the big house behind our window box?"

Mr. McTwiddle always answered, "Nothing that would interest you, Tiny. Isn't it pleasant to be as snug as a bug in a rug, here in our little cookie carton?"

And they all agreed that it was.

Each day at breakfast Tessie asked, "What's
inside the big house behind our window box?"

Mrs. McTwiddle always answered, "Nothing
that would interest you, Tessie. Isn't it nice to be
safe and cozy here in our own little cookie
carton?"

And they all agreed that it was.

One sunny morning Tessie said to Tiny, "I want to see for myself what's inside the big house." And since Tiny wanted to do everything Tessie did, they both flew up to the windowsill.

"Oh, look!" Tessie cried as they peered through the window and saw a dollhouse. "That beautiful house must be meant for Twiddlebugs. It's just our size!"

They flew through a crack at the top of the window to take a closer look.

"Oh, look at those soft armchairs!" cried Tiny.
"They're not like those hard corks we sit on."
"And I bet the beds are more comfy than
matchboxes," said Tessie. "I want to live here!"

Tiny and Tessie talked and dreamed of nothing but living in the fine house.

That night at bedtime Mr. McTwiddle said, "Isn't it pleasant to be as snug as a bug in a rug, here in our own little cookie carton?"

Only Mrs. McTwiddle agreed that it was.

The next day Tiny and Tessie coaxed and pleaded until at last Mr. and Mrs. McTwiddle gave in. The family packed up a few things and moved to the dollhouse.

"You were right, children," said Mr. McTwiddle. "What a comfortable chair!"

"Whoopee!" called Tiny from the bathroom.
"Now Rubber Duckie and I can take a bubble bath
in a real bathtub."

"This is a Twiddle-dream come true!" said
Mrs. McTwiddle as she tucked Tessie in.
And they all agreed that it was.

The next morning, after the McTwiddles had gone back to the window box to tend their garden, the little girl who lived in the big house came to play with her dollhouse.

"Hmm. The beds would look better downstairs," Jane said to herself. "And the armchairs would look better upstairs."

And she moved all the furniture around.

When the Twiddlebugs returned to the house
that night, they were astonished.

"My goodness," said Mrs. McTwiddle, "where is
my stove?"

"My goodness," said Mr. McTwiddle, "there's a
stove where my armchair used to be!"

"I'm sure the refrigerator wasn't in the
bathroom this morning," said Tiny.

"Why is the quilt on the floor?" wondered Tessie.
"This is very mysterious," said Mr. McTwiddle.
But the McTwiddles stayed on in the new house.

The next day while the
McTwiddles were away,
Jane's friend Sally came over
for a tea party.

"Let's move the dollhouse
out of the way," said Jane.
"Try to be careful, so nothing
falls out."

What a mess the McTwiddles came back to that night!

"Nothing like this ever happened in our old cookie carton," Mrs. McTwiddle wailed.

Tessie started to cry. "This house isn't so wonderful after all," she sniffed, turning a chair right side up again.

And they all agreed that it wasn't.

When everything was back in place, the exhausted Twiddlebugs went right to bed. But Mr. McTwiddle couldn't sleep. He had a feeling that something awful was about to happen.

Suddenly a fat, furry leg darted in the window. Then a fat, furry paw landed right on him.

"Eeeek!" he screamed. "There's a monster trying to get in!"

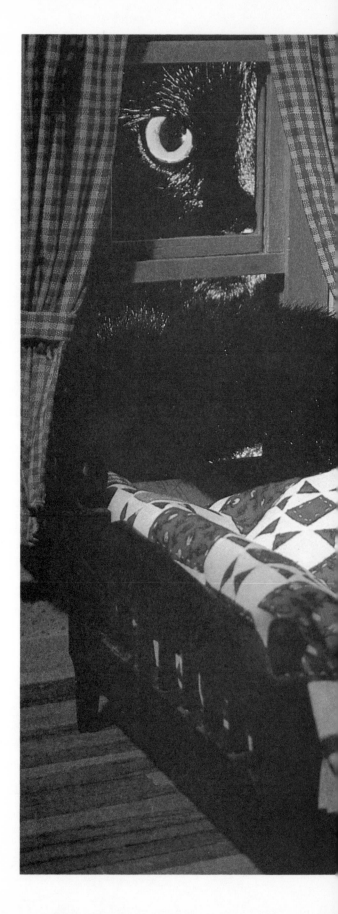

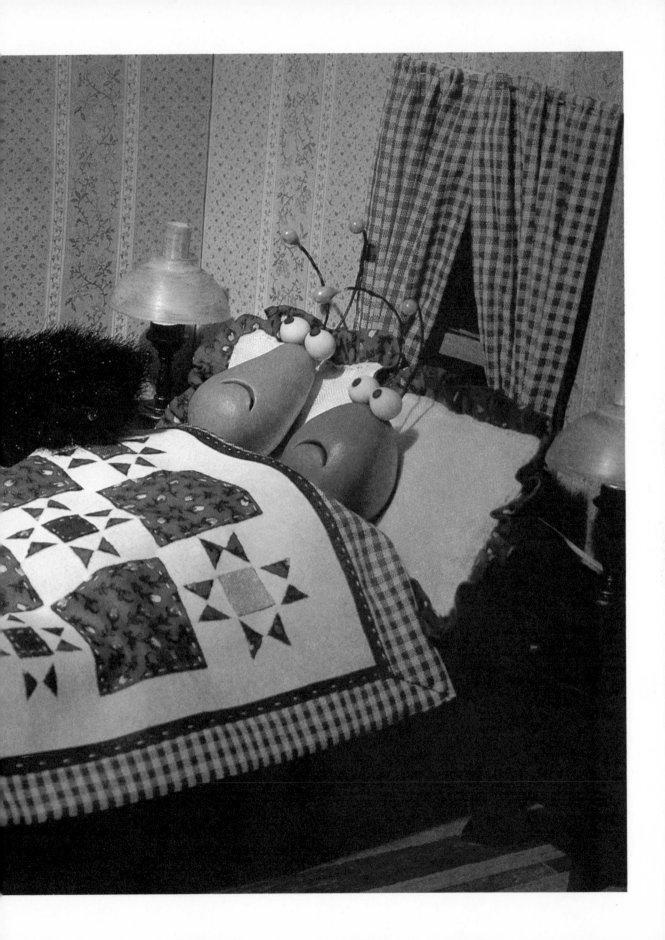

"Oh, no!" shrieked Mrs. McTwiddle. "This house isn't safe!"

"I want to go home," cried Tessie.

"Me, too!" said Tiny.

"We're going back to the window box, where we belong," said Mr. McTwiddle.

They quickly packed up their things.

In two flits of a
Twiddlebug's wing, the
McTwiddles were back in
their old home. They hopped
into their matchbox beds and
pulled the covers up tight.

"Now," said Mr. McTwiddle,
"isn't it nice to be snug as a
bug in a rug, in our own cozy
cookie carton?"

And this time, they all
agreed that it was!